# The Frog Prince Continued

STORY BY JON SCIESZKA

PAINTINGS BY STEVE JOHNSON

A TRUMPET CLUB SPECIAL EDITION

Published by The Trumpet Club
666 Fifth Avenue, New York, New York 10103

Text copyright © Jon Scieszka, 1991
Illustrations copyright © Steve Johnson, 1991

All rights reserved. No part of this book may be reproduced or transmitted in any
form or by any means, electronic or mechanical, including photocopying, recording or
by any information storage and retrieval system, without the written permission of the
Publisher, except where permitted by law. For information address: Viking Penguin,
a division of Penguin Books USA Inc., New York, New York.

ISBN 0-440-84446-0

This edition published by arrangement with Viking Penguin,
a division of Penguin Books USA Inc.

Set in 16 point Caledonia

Book design and art direction by Lou Fancher with Jeri Hansen

Printed in the United States of America
October 1992

1 3 5 7 9 10 8 6 4 2

DAN

*To Mom and Dad*
JS

*To our Grandparents
for cookies, tree climbing,
dancing, and frog hunts.*
SJ and LF

The Princess kissed the frog.

He turned into a prince.

And they lived happily ever after...

ell, let's just say they lived sort of

happily for a long time.

Okay, so they weren't so happy.

In fact, they were miserable.

"Stop sticking your tongue out like that,"
nagged the Princess.

"How come you never want to go down to
the pond anymore?" whined the Prince.

The Prince and Princess were so unhappy.

They didn't know what to do.

"I would prefer that you not hop around on the furniture," said the Princess. "And it might be nice if you got out of the castle once in a while to slay a dragon or giant or whatever."

The Prince didn't feel like going out and slaying anything.

He just felt like running away. But then he reread his book. And it said right there at the end of his story: "They lived happily ever after. The End."

So he stayed in the castle and drove the Princess crazy.

Then one day, the Princess threw a perfectly awful fit.

"First you keep me awake all night with your horrible, croaking snore. Now I find a lily pad in your pocket. I can't believe I actually kissed your slimy frog lips. Sometimes I think we would both be better off if you were still a frog."

That's when the idea hit him.

The Prince thought. "Still a frog . . . Yes! That's it!"

And he ran off into the forest, looking for a witch

who could turn him back into a frog.

The Prince hadn't gone far when he ran into just the person he was looking for.

"Miss Witch, Miss Witch. Excuse me, Miss Witch. I wonder if you could help me?"

"Say, you're not looking for a princess to kiss are you?" asked the witch.

"Oh, no. I've already been kissed. I'm the Frog Prince. Actually, I was hoping you could turn me back into a frog."

"Are you sure you're not looking for a beautiful sleeping princess to kiss and wake up?"

"No, no—I'm the Frog Prince."

"That's funny. You don't look like a frog.
Well, no matter. If you're a prince, you're a prince.
And I'll have to cast a nasty spell on you.
I can't have any princes waking up Sleeping Beauty
before the hundred years are up."

The Prince didn't stick around to see which nasty
spell the witch had in mind. He ran deeper
into the forest until he came to a tiny cottage where
he saw another lady who might help him.

"Miss Witch, Miss Witch. Excuse me, Miss Witch. I wonder if you could help me. I'm a prince and—"

"Eh? What did you say? Prince?" croaked the witch.

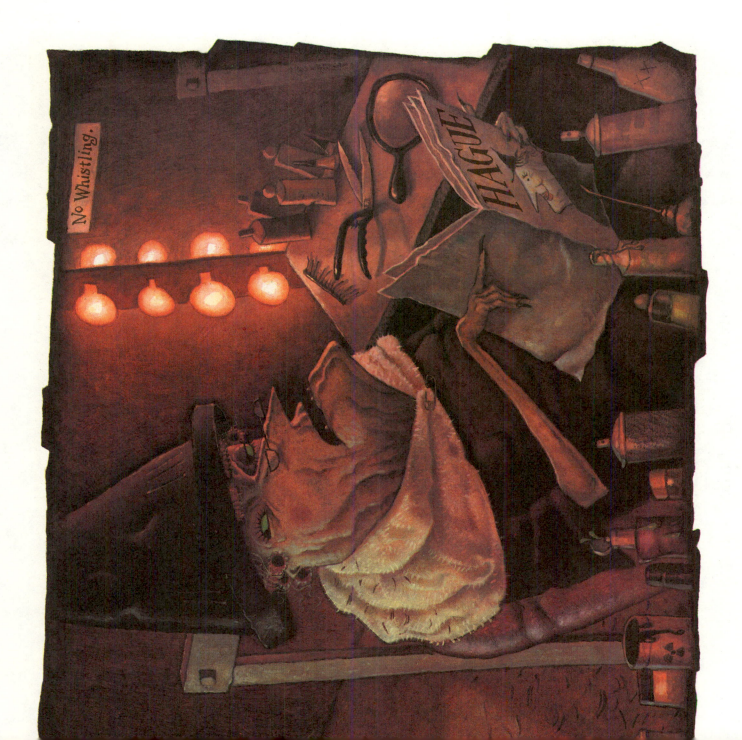

"No. I mean, yes. I mean, no, I'm not the prince looking for Sleeping Beauty. But, yes, I'm the Frog Prince. And I'm looking for a member of your profession who can turn me back into a frog so I can live happily ever after."

"Frog Prince, you say? That's funny, I thought frogs were little green guys with webbed feet. Well, no matter. If you're a prince, you're a prince. And I can't have any princes rescuing Snow White. Here—eat the rest of this apple."

The Prince, who knew his fairy tales (and knew a poisoned apple when he saw one), didn't even stay to say, "No, thank you." He turned and ran deeper into the forest. Soon he came to a strange-looking house with a witch outside.

"*Ahem.* Miss Witch, Miss Witch. Excuse me, Miss Witch. I wonder if you could help me? I'm the Frog—"

"If you're a frog, I'm the King of France," said the witch.

"No, I'm not a frog. I'm the Frog Prince. But I need a witch to turn me back into a frog so I can

live happily ever after can you do it?" said the Prince in one long breath.

The witch eyed the Prince and licked her rather plump lips.

"Why, of course, dearie. Come right in. Maybe I can fit you in for lunch."

The Prince stopped on the slightly gummy steps. Something about this house seemed very familiar. He broke off a corner of the windowsill and tasted it. Gingerbread.

"I hope you don't mind my asking, Miss Witch. But do you happen to know any children by the name of Hansel and Gretel?"

"Why yes, Prince darling, I do. I'm expecting them for dinner."

The Prince, who, as we said before, knew his fairy tales, ran as fast as he could deeper into the forest.

Soon he was completely lost.

He saw someone standing next to a tree. The Prince walked up to her, hoping she wasn't a witch, for he'd quite had his fill of witches.

"Madam. I am the Frog Prince. Could you help me?"

"Gosh, do you need it," said the Fairy Godmother. "You are the worst-looking frog I've ever seen."

"I am not a frog. I am the Frog Prince," said the Prince, getting a little annoyed. "And I need someone to turn me back into a frog so I can live happily ever after."

"Well, I'm on my way to see a girl in the village about going to a ball, but I suppose I could give it a try. I've never done frogs before, you know."

And with that the Fairy Godmother waved her magic wand, and turned the Prince into a beautiful . . .

carriage.
The Prince couldn't believe his rotten luck.

The sun went down. The forest got spookier.
And the Prince became more and more frightened.

Oh, what an idiot I've been. I could be sitting at home with the Princess, living happily ever after. But instead, I'm stuck here in the middle of this stupid forest, turned into a stupid carriage. Now I'll probably just rot and fall apart and live unhappily ever after."

The Prince thought these terrible, frightening kinds of thoughts (and a few worse—too awful to tell), until far away in the village, the clock struck midnight.

The Carriage instantly turned back into his former Prince self, and ran by the light of the moon until he was safe inside his own castle.

"Where have you been? I've been worried sick. You're seven hours late. Your dinner is cold. Your clothes are a mess."

The Prince looked at the Princess who had believed him when no one else in the world had, the Princess who had actually kissed his slimy frog lips. The Princess who loved him.

*The Prince kissed the Princess.*
*They both turned into frogs.*
*And they hopped off happily ever after.*

The End.